To Princess Dodo and Prince Guff

with love

T.M.

ORCHARD BOOKS
96 Leonard Street, London EC2A 4RH
Orchard Books Australia
14 Mars Road, Lane Cove, NSW 2066
First published in Great Britain 1996
First paperback publication 1997
Text © Tony Mitton 1996
Illustrations © Martin Chatterton 1996
The right of Tony Mitton to be identified as the Author
and Martin Chatterton as the Illustrator of this Work
has been asserted by them in accordance with
the Copyright, Designs and Patents Act, 1988.
A CIP catalogue record for this book is available
from the British Library.
1 86039 152 4 (hardback)
1 86039 366 7 (paperback)
Printed in Great Britain

Royal Raps

Tony Mitton

Illustrated by Martin Chatterton

 ORCHARD BOOKS

Collect these Rap Rhymes!

Big Bad Raps

Royal Raps

Contents

Cinderella

Rap

I'm gonna tell a story
'bout a girl I know.
The whole thing happened
a long time ago.
She lived with her stepmother
(cruel and mean)
and the nastiest sisters
there've ever been.

Now these two sisters
and that mean old mum,
they treated Cinderella
like she was dumb.
They fed her on scraps,

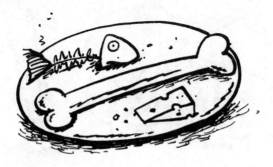

gave her rags to wear.

They bossed her about
and it just wasn't fair.

They got her to clean
and they made her cook,
but they hardly ever gave her
a word or a look
except to say,
"Hey there,
Sis, come here…
Do this and do that
and now – disappear!"

And that's about the way
her life went by
with hardly the time
for a sob or a sigh.
Until one day
with a RAT-TAT-TAT
a golden invitation card
dropped on the mat.

Cinderella listened
while Stepma read,
and these are the words
that the invite said:

Prince Charming has reached
that time in life
When a prince oughta settle down
and find a wife.
And if the girl he wants
agrees and says "Yes!"
then she's gonna be
our new princess.
So if you wanna sit
on a royal throne,
don't stay at home
watching TV alone
Dress yourself up
in your very best frock
And come to the palace
at 8 o'clock
Make sure that you get here.
Don't miss this chance.
"It COULD BE YOU!"
at the Engagement Dance.

"Oh, Mama, dear Mama,"
said Sister One,
"I'll go in my red dress.
This sounds like fun."

"Oh, yes, dear Mama,"
said Sister Two,
"I'll dye my hair pink
and go in blue."

12

"Oh, Mama, please, Mama,"
said young Cinderella,
"I guess Prince Charming
is a real nice fella.
I know that a Prince
wouldn't want to marry me,
but maybe, please, Mama,
I could just go see...?"

"Well, really, Cinderella,
it's not for you.
You haven't the time.
You've work to do.
We need to get ready.
We want to look nice.
Get back to your kitchen,
I won't tell you twice."

The evening came round
in no time at all,
and everyone went
to the Royal Ball.

So Cinderella wept
as she did the dirty dishes,
but while she washed up
she dreamed up wishes.

"OK, honey,"
said a real sweet voice.
"High-fashion dress
and a white Rolls-Royce?
It ain't no trouble
to a Mama like me.
I got the magic.
Just watch and see!"
And there, right in front of her,
Cinderella saw
a big Fairy Mama
at the kitchen door.

"I'll fix your wishes, honey,
don't you worry.
But there ain't much time,
so the word is – hurry!"
She snatched a dirty saucepan
and flung it at a rat,
cried "ALA KAZAM!"
and that was that:

The rat turned chauffeur,
the saucepan shone clean
and stretched itself into
a long limousine.

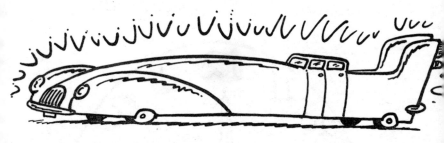

And Cinderella stood there
in a beautiful gown.
"Driver!" said the Mama,
"Take her to Town.

But make sure you're back
before midnight's here,
'cos all this magic's
gonna disappear."

Well, telling it quickly,
and telling it straight,
Cinderella went
and she stayed till late.

She danced with the Prince
and her wish came true.
He smiled and he said,
"Cindie, baby, it's you…"

They stopped for a burger
and a bubbly drink,
when Cinderella's digital
began to twink.

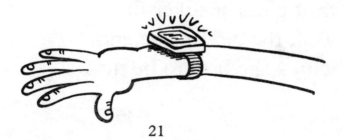

Cinderella vanished,
and all the Prince found
was a small glass sneaker
lying on the ground.

But the Prince wasn't beaten.
He gave a command
to drive that sneaker
all around the land.
And when they found the foot
that glass sneaker fit,
well, the girl on the end,
why – she had to be it.

Well, let me reassure you
that it didn't take long.
For, after all, a magic sneaker
can't go wrong.
Everyone tried it.
Everybody failed.

The first sister wept

and the second one wailed.

But Cinderella's foot fit
neat as a glove.
And that was the start
of a sole-ful love.

So that's how Cinderella
got to get her wishes –
a life at the Palace
and no more dishes.
(Except that the Prince
is a bit of a dish.
He's the hunkiest guy
that a girl could wish.)

But back at home her sisters
are down on all fours,
sweeping up the dust
and polishing the floors.
And Stepma's had to learn
to sew and to mend,
so she can stitch the story up –
this is the end.

Back in the past
lived a little princess
with a real cute face
and a fancy dress.

She was kinda fussy
(if you know what I mean)
'cos she knew that one day
she was gonna be a queen.
Well, her family was rich.
(Her Daddy was King.)
So the princess had
'most everything.

But out of her toys
what she loved most of all
was a tiny, shiny
golden ball.
She carried it almost
everywhere
to hold in her hand
and throw in the air.
But one day she threw it
a bit too high.
The ball flew up
in the big blue sky.

She held out her hand
but it fell beyond,
and it landed PLOP!
in the garden pond.
Well, the pond was dirty,
the pond was deep,
so the little princess
began to weep.
"Hey, now!" said a voice
from a bush close by.

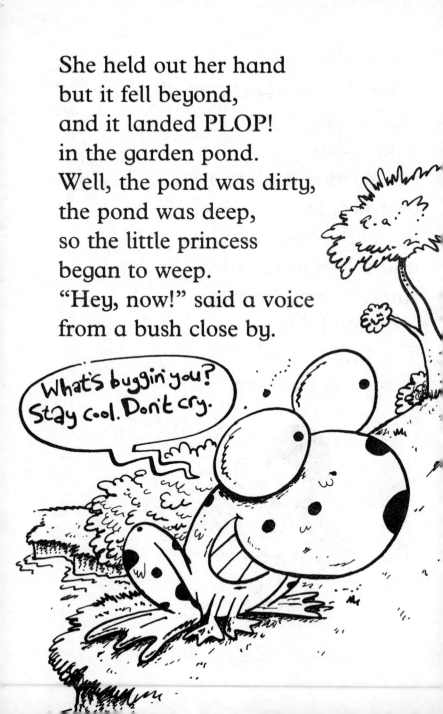

The princess looked,
said,

"I'm a frog, as it happens,"
the small voice spoke.
"Anybody knows
that toads don't croak.
But I heard you crying
and you look real blue.

Is there something, maybe,
that I can do?"
So the princess told him
about the ball.
"Easy," he croaked.
"No trouble at all.
But a frog can't afford
to do things for free.
If I get it out
what's in it for me?"

Said the princess,

The frog got the ball,
yes, he fetched it quick.
"Oh, thanks," said the princess.
"Now take your pick.

You can have my dresses,
you can have my rings,
you can choose what you like
from my fancy things."
But the frog took a breath,
then he gave a sigh.
He puffed his throat
and he blinked an eye,

Don't want your stuff
I wanna be your mate.
Wanna sit in your lap
and eat from your plate.

"Wanna be your friend,
wanna share your bed.
Wanna lie on your pillow
close to your head."
"Oh, yuck!" screamed the
princess.

She stamped her foot
and she stormed away
as the frog looked after her
in dismay.
He saw her shudder
and toss her head,
as she went off to play
with her hamster, instead.

But round about teatime
as she sat down to eat,
came a slip, slop, slopping
of slippery feet.
Her Daddy gave a frown
as he put down his tea.
Said, "Listen to that, dear.
What can it be?"

Then the princess blushed
and began to wail.
She told her Daddy
the whole darn tale.

"I'm sorry my dear,"
said the king with a frown.
And he sighed a sigh
as he scratched his crown.

So he opened the door
to the slippery chap,
and quick as a flash
he was in her lap.
Then he jumped on up
and he perched on her plate,
and she nearly choked
with each bite she ate.

But the frog stayed with her,
whatever she tried.
He stayed real close
and just smiled and sighed.
He sat on her shoulder
for 'toons on telly.
The princess thought,
"This dude is smelly!"

She got out her homework
and tried not to look,
but the frog went hopping
all round her book.

Then the maid came by.
"Oh, Miss," she said,
"your Mama says
it's time for bed."

And the princess thought,
"I'll never get to sleep
if I share my bed
with this slippery creep!"
But what could she do?
So she shook her head
and the frog hopped with her
up to bed.

She was cleaning her teeth
at the bedroom sink,
when she heard a noise –
and what do you think?

That frog was growing...

bigger and bigger.

His face was changing
and so was his figure!
She put down the brush,
took a quick rinse –
and the frog had become

a handsome prince!

The prince gave a gulp
and then he spoke.
(His voice had almost
lost its croak.)
"A rebbitle spell...
I mean...terrible, sister,
'cos I ain't a frog,
I'm a royal mister.

46

I blew my cool,
got rude to a witch,
had to do my time
in a slimy ditch,
had to hop around
in a green frog skin
till a pretty princess
took me in.

Yes, I'd still be stuck
on a lily pad
if it wasn't for you
and your dear old Dad.
So maybe now
we can really be friends…"
(and that's the place
this story ends –

except to say
that I hope y'all
gonna come to the wedding.
It's a Hip-Hop Ball!)